Karl Malone

PHOTO CREDITS
The National Basketball Association
Nathaniel S. Butler: Cover, pg. 26 and 29
Andrew D. Bernstein: pg. 2, 3, 6, 9, 10, 14, 17, 18, 22, 25 and 30
Barry Gossage: pg. 13 and 21

Text copyright © 1993 by The Child's World, Inc.
All rights reserved. No part of this book may be
reproduced or utilized in any form or by any means
without written permission from the Publisher.
Printed in the United States of America.

Distributed to Schools and Libraries
in the United States by
ENCYCLOPAEDIA BRITANNICA EDUCATIONAL CORP.
310 S. Michigan Avenue
Chicago, Illinois 60604

Library of Congress Cataloging-in-Publication Data
Rambeck, Richard.
Karl Malone / Richard Rambeck.
p. cm.
Summary: A career biography of power forward in the
National Basketball Association, Karl Malone.
ISBN 0-89565-961-1
1. Malone, Karl—Juvenile literature.
2. Basketball players—United States—Biography—Juvenile literature.
[1. Malone, Karl. 2. Basketball players. 3. Afro-Americans—Biography.]
I. Title.
GV884.M18R36 1993   92-6586
796.323092–dc20   CIP
[B]   AC

Karl Malone

by Richard Rambeck

Warsaw Community Public Library
310 East Main Street
Warsaw, IN 46580
219-267-6011

The Mailman delivers again.

Lucas Learns a Lesson

Maurice Lucas wasn't happy. In fact, he was angry. Lucas, one of the best power forwards in the history of the National Basketball Association, wasn't having a good night. Lucas wasn't getting a lot of rebounds. He wasn't able to score much either. Every time Lucas jumped to get a rebound, it seemed someone else had beaten him to the ball. That someone else was Karl Malone. Malone, who was only a rookie, was teaching the veteran Lucas a lesson. But Lucas was used to being the teacher.

'Stop Going Over Me'

Finally, Lucas couldn't take it anymore. After Malone outjumped him for a rebound, Lucas turned on the rookie and glared. "Stop going over me," Lucas warned, "before I hurt you." The veteran was trying to scare Malone–something Lucas had been doing to other NBA power forwards for almost ten years. Malone merely looked at Lucas, and said nothing. A couple minutes later, Malone's Utah Jazz had a fast break. Malone got the ball and drove to the basket. Maurice Lucas stood in the way.

Scoring against the Lakers.

Karl zeros in on the basket.

Nobody Scares Karl Malone

"**S**top going over me before I hurt you." Malone didn't stop. He just kept going up–and over Lucas. The Utah rookie then hammered down a powerful dunk. Right in Lucas' face. "Nobody," Malone recalled a couple of years later, "has tried to scare me since." That's not surprising, because it's hard to imagine anyone actually scaring Karl Malone. He is six-feet-nine and weighs 256 pounds. Malone looks like a bodybuilder, but he has the speed of a sprinter. Not only that, it seems as if Karl can go on running and playing forever.

"He's on a Different Standard"

"I've never seen Karl tired," said Utah point-guard John Stockton. "He's on a different standard than the rest of us." Former Utah coach Frank Layden said Malone could play 200 games a year if he had to. "He gets stronger as the season goes on," Layden claimed. The reason is that Malone is always pushing himself to do better, to do more. Every morning, he gets up and does 400 sit-ups. Then he does ten 100-meter dashes, followed by three 200-meter runs and three 300-meter runs.

"Biggest heart in Utah."

"This ball is mine."

Loves Lifting Weights

That would be enough to tire out most athletes, but Malone is just getting started. Next, he goes into the weight room in his Salt Lake City home and builds his incredible body. "I like doing it," he explained. "I see myself improving. I feel the power and strength growing." Malone may be the only basketball player in history who looks like Mr. Universe. Utah teammate Scott Roth couldn't believe how hard Malone worked out. "That man has to be one of the most magnificent athletes on the face of the earth," Roth said.

Size, Strength and Speed

Malone has built himself into one of the finest players in the NBA. Many experts believe he is the best power forward in the league. That's because Malone has the strength and size of a center and the speed of a guard. "He runs the court like a small man, then he overpowers bigger people," said Golden State coach Don Nelson. "Is there a more dominant power forward in the game today? If there is, I'd like to see him." Malone may have become an NBA all-star, but he still hasn't forgotten where he came from.

Super-strong superstar.

A dunk from the Mailman.

Family Didn't Have Much Money

Karl Malone and eight brothers and sisters grew up in Summerfield, Louisiana. The town had a population of about 150. Most of the people in Summerfield were poor, including Karl's family. His mother, Shirley Turner, had to work two jobs to support her family. Shirley would go to the town sawmill in the morning. Then she would leave in the afternoon for another job where she cut up chickens so the meat could be sent to supermarkets. Despite Shirley's two jobs, there wasn't much money for Karl and his brothers and sisters.

"I Can Never Repay Her"

"I saw my mother wear cardboard in her shoes, just so each of us could have a good pair of shoes," Karl recalled. "I saw what the water did to that cardboard. My mother did so much for us. I can never repay her." But Karl certainly has tried. He grew to be tall and strong. He also was a great basketball player. Malone got a scholarship offer from nearby Louisiana Tech. He played there for three years before deciding to turn pro. Karl might have stayed in school for his senior year, but he wanted to earn money to help support his mother and family.

Karl rules the inside.

1985 first-round draft choice.

Utah Gets the "Mailman"

Malone left Louisiana Tech after his junior year. He had led the team to the NCAA tournament, but he knew it was time to move on. The Utah Jazz picked the powerful Malone in the first round of the 1985 draft. The Jazz had drafted a forward whose nickname was the "Mailman," because, no matter what, Karl Malone always delivered. The Mailman joined a club that was on its way up. Malone and little John Stockton teamed up to make a great pair. Stockton ran the offense. Malone grabbed the rebounds and scored a lot of points.

Sweet Music for the Jazz

During the 1987-88 season, the Jazz rolled to a 47-35 record, best in team history. One of the main reasons was Karl Malone. The Mailman averaged 27.7 points and 12.0 rebounds per game. Malone led the Jazz in scoring in sixty-three of eighty-two games. He also topped the team in rebounding fifty-nine times during the 1987-88 season. But Malone saved his best for the playoffs. In the Western Conference semifinals, the Jazz battled the Lakers in a great series. Malone averaged twenty-nine points and twelve rebounds per game in the series. But Utah still lost.

Malone battles the Lakers.

Working hard to be the best.

Working Hard, Paying the Price

After that series, most of the experts agreed that Karl Malone was the best power forward in the league. But Malone himself wasn't sure. He knew he could be the best in the league, but he wanted to be the best all the time, every game. "All I can do is work and perform," he explained. "I'm always thinking, Have I paid the price to be here? Have I worked hard enough? Do I deserve to be the Mailman?" So Malone kept on working as hard as he could to get better. He worked at trying to improve the weak points of his game.

Improvement at the Foul Line

One of Karl Malone's weaknesses was free-throw shooting. When he came into the NBA, Malone was not a good foul shooter. He made only about sixty percent from the line. Not only that, Malone got fouled a lot. So he went to the line often, and he often missed. "I have to shoot my free throws better," Malone said early in his career. So when he wasn't lifting weights or running up and down hills, the Mailman was practicing free throws. During the 1989-90 season, Malone made almost seventy-seven percent of his foul shots. The Mailman had delivered again.

Delivering at the foul line.

Standing up to anybody.

"Biggest Heart in Utah"

Karl Malone delivers on the court, but he also delivers off the court. When Scott Roth was trying to earn a place on Utah's roster, Malone let Roth move in with him. Roth made the team, and he wound up staying with Malone all season. "The man," Roth said, "has the biggest heart in Utah." It's Malone's heart that makes him special. It's his heart that makes him work so hard. It's his heart that makes him stand up to anyone on the court. It doesn't matter whether it's Maurice Lucas, or Charles Barkley, or Larry Bird. The Mailman has to deliver–no matter what.